In memory of Our Doris, my fantastic mum
and for Jane, wonderful mother of our children.
A.B

MY MUM
A PICTURE CORGI BOOK 978 0 552 56020 7

First published in Great Britain by Doubleday,
an imprint of Random House Children's Books
A Random House Group Company

Doubleday edition published 2005
Picture Corgi edition published 2006
This Picture Corgi edition published 2010

1 3 5 7 9 10 8 6 4 2

Set in Goudy Old Style

Picture Corgi Books are published by Random House Children's Books,
61–63 Uxbridge Road, London W5 5SA

www.**kidsatrandomhouse**.co.uk
www.**rbooks**.co.uk

Addresses for companies within The Random House Group Limited
can be found at: www.randomhouse.co.uk/offices.htm

THE RANDOM HOUSE GROUP Limited Reg. No. 954009

A CIP catalogue record for this book is
available from the British Library.

Printed in Singapore

My Mum

Anthony Browne

Picture Corgi

She's nice, my mum.

My *mum's a fantastic cook,*

and a brilliant juggler.

She's a great painter,

and the STRONGEST woman in the world!

She's really nice, my mum.

My mum's a magic gardener.
She can make ANYTHING grow.

And she's a good fairy.
When I'm sad she can make me happy.

She can sing like an angel,

and roar like a lion.

She's really, REALLY nice, my mum.

My mum's as beautiful as a butterfly,

and as comfy
as an
armchair.

She's as soft as a kitten,

and as tough as a rhino.

She's really, REALLY,
REALLY *nice, my mum.*

My mum could be a dancer,

or an astronaut.

She could be a film star,

or the big boss. But she's MY mum.

She's a SUPERMUM!

And she makes me laugh. A lot.

I love my mum.

And you know what?

SHE LOVES ME!

(And she always will.)